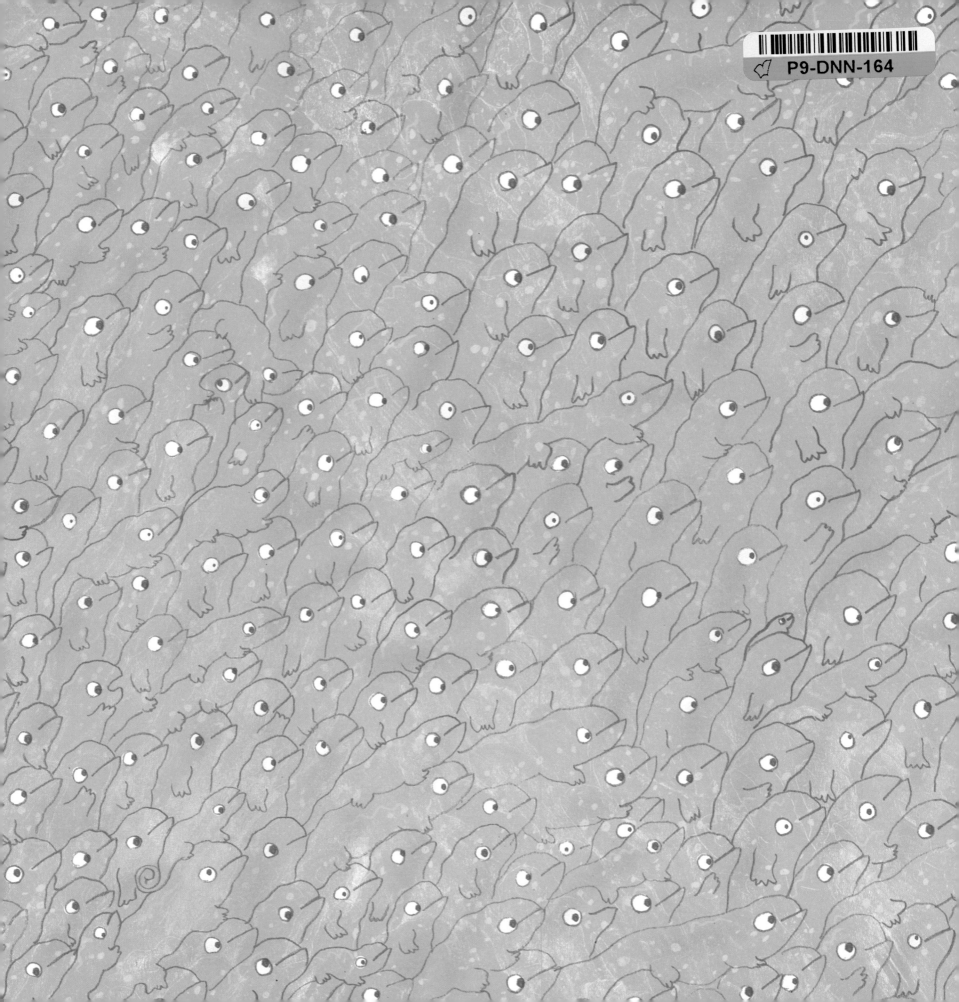

To my brothers, Kev, Rich, and Andy

All rights reserved. Published by Scholastic Press, an imprint of Scholastic Inc.,
Publishers since 1920. SCHOLASTIC, SCHOLASTIC PRESS, and associated logos are trademarks
and/or registered trademarks of Scholastic Inc.

Published in 2015 by Hodder Children's Books, an imprint of Hachette Children's Books,
an Hachette UK company.

Library of Congress Cataloging-in-Publication Data Available

ISBN 978-0-545-84902-9

10 9 8 7 6 5 4 3 2 1   15 16 17 18 19

Printed in China   54
First edition, November 2015

GREEN LIZARDS
VS.
RED RECTANGLES

Steve Antony

Scholastic Press • New York

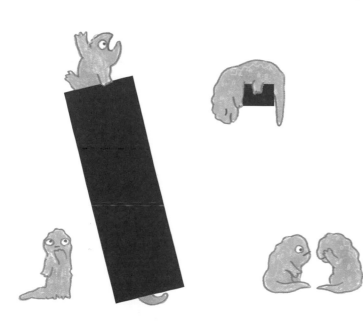

The **GREEN LIZARDS** and the
RED RECTANGLES were at war.

The **GREEN LIZARDS** tried their best to defeat the **RED RECTANGLES,**

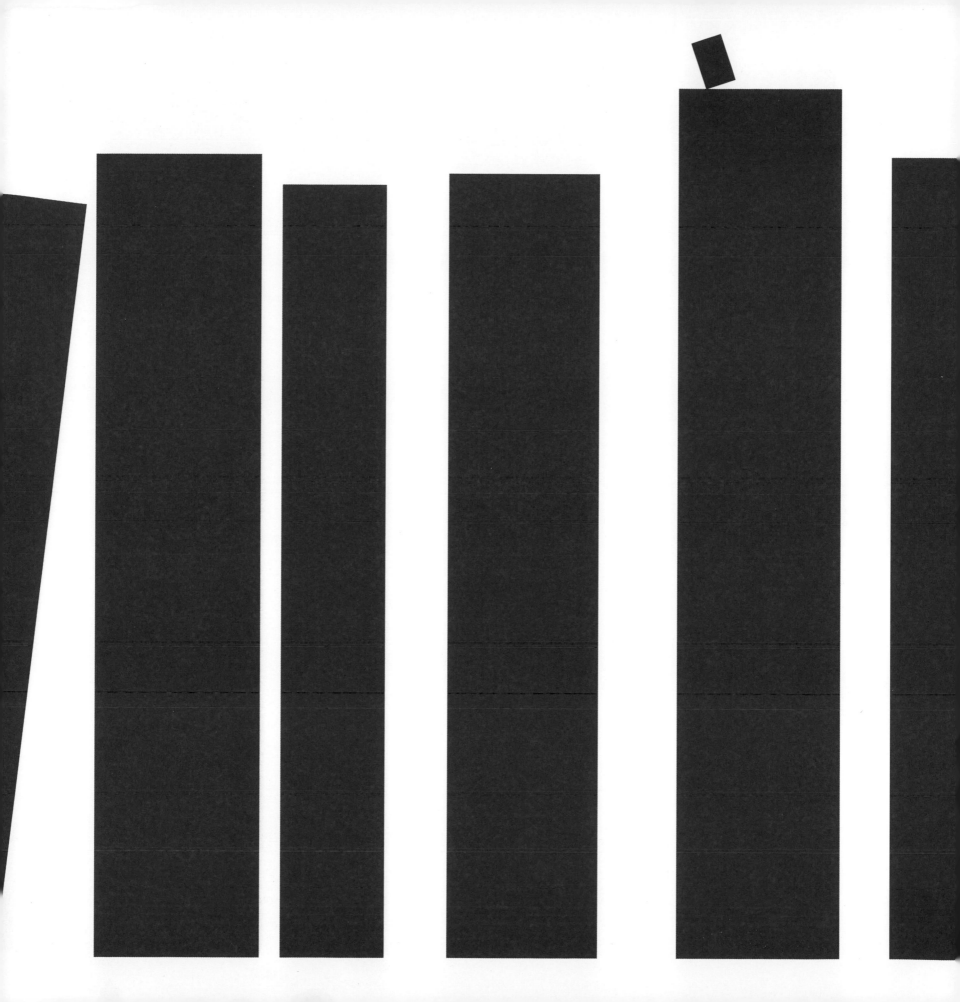

but the
**RED
RECTANGLES**
were smart.

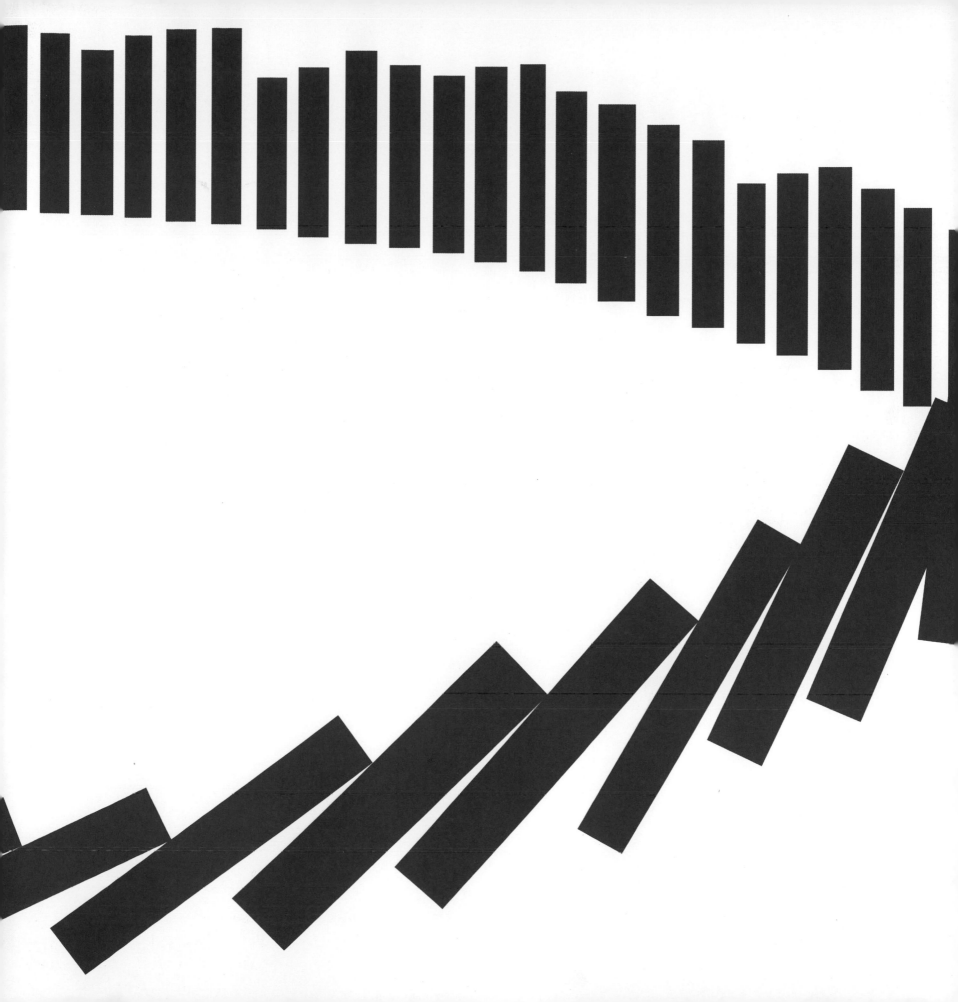

The **RED RECTANGLES** tried their best to defeat

the **GREEN LIZARDS,**

but the **GREEN LIZARDS** were strong.

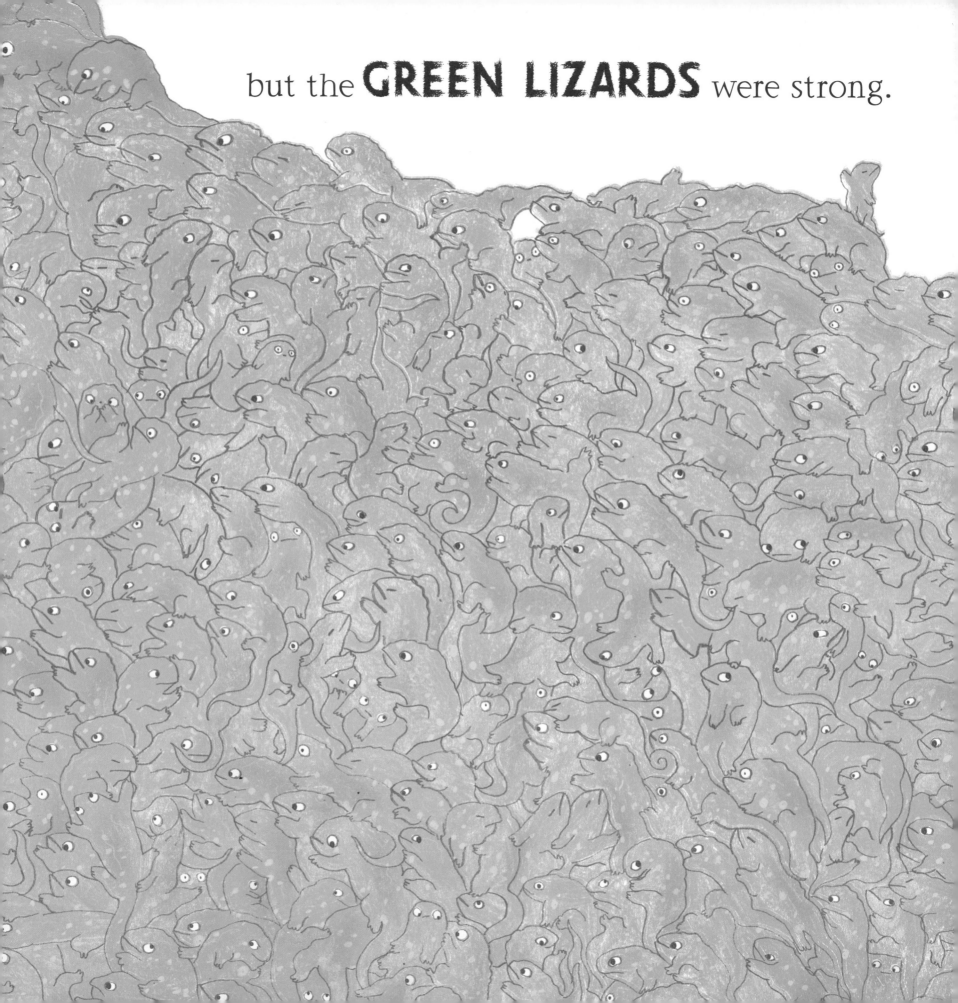

WHAT ARE WE FIGHTING FOR?

asked one **GREEN LIZARD.**

But he was SQUASHED, and this led to...

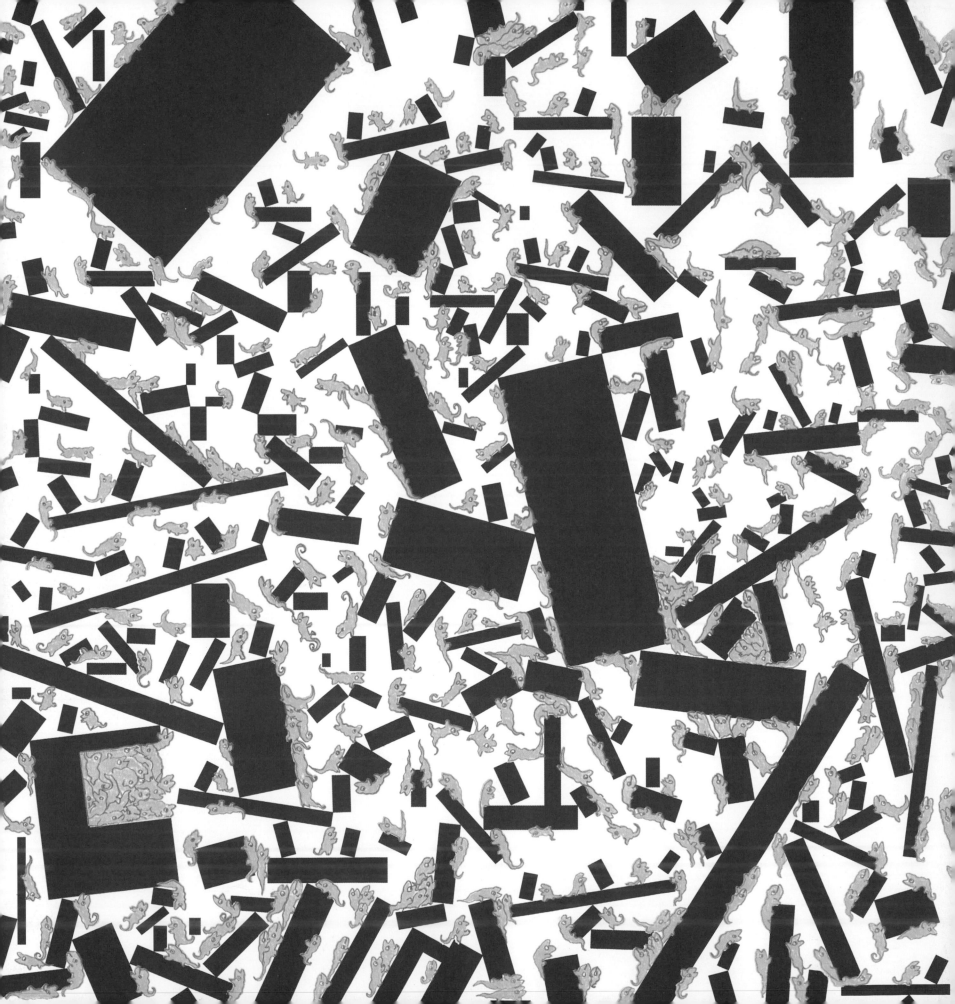

and fought and fought until...

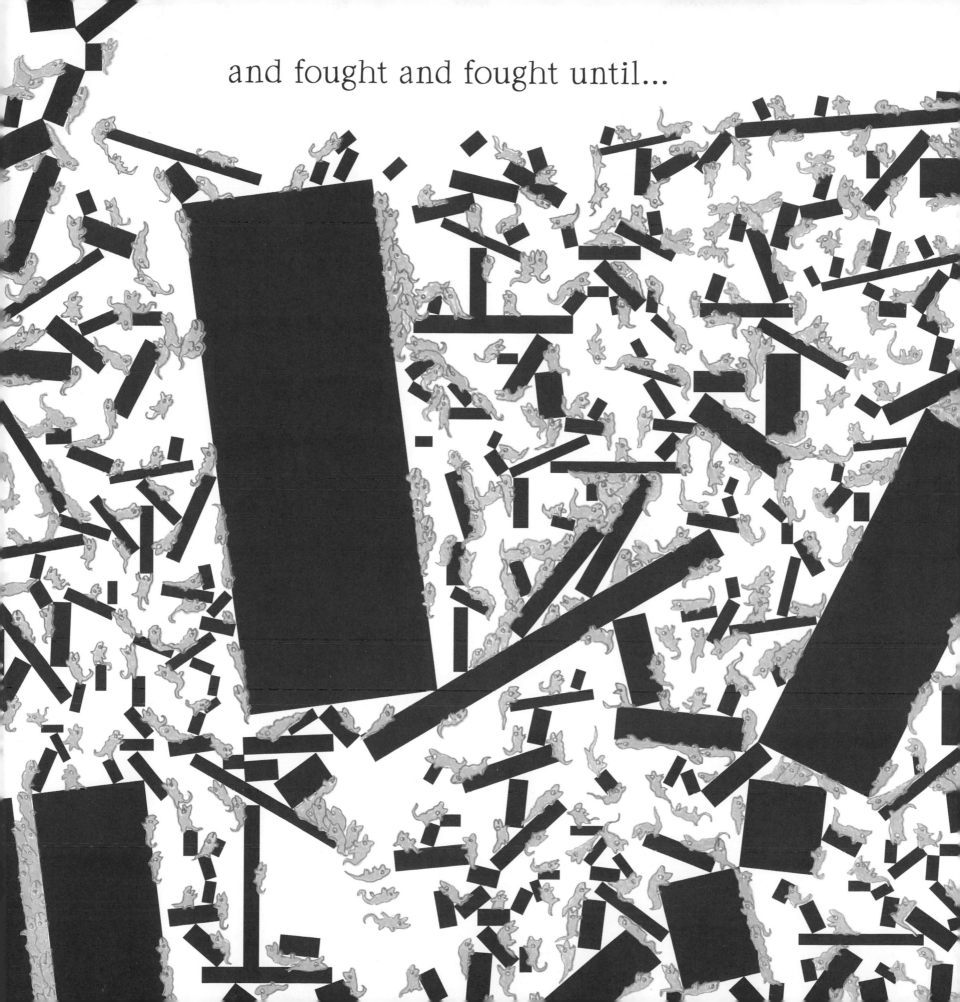

they could fight no more.

The **GREEN LIZARDS** and the **RED RECTANGLES** gathered for a truce, and finally they found a way...

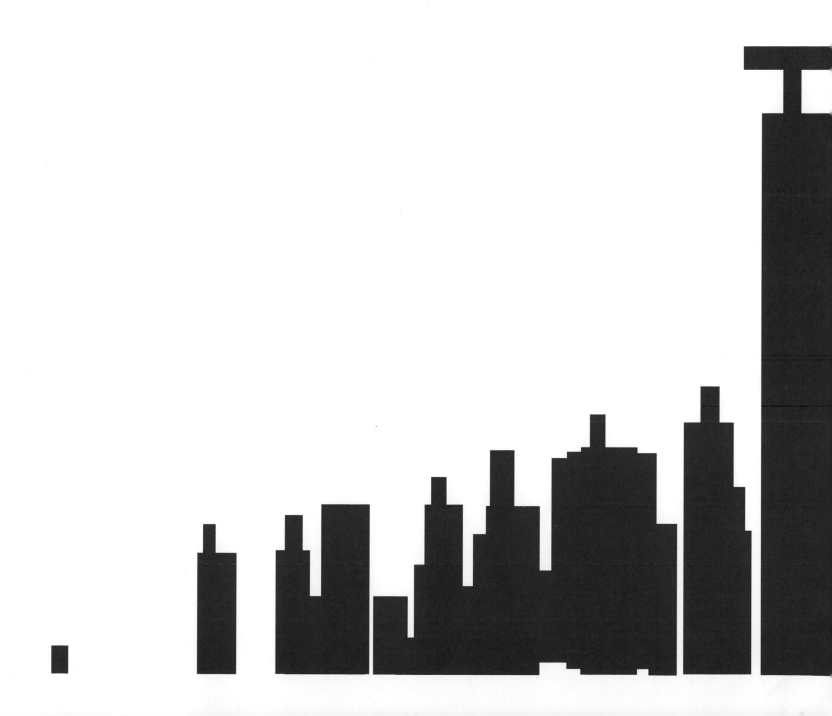

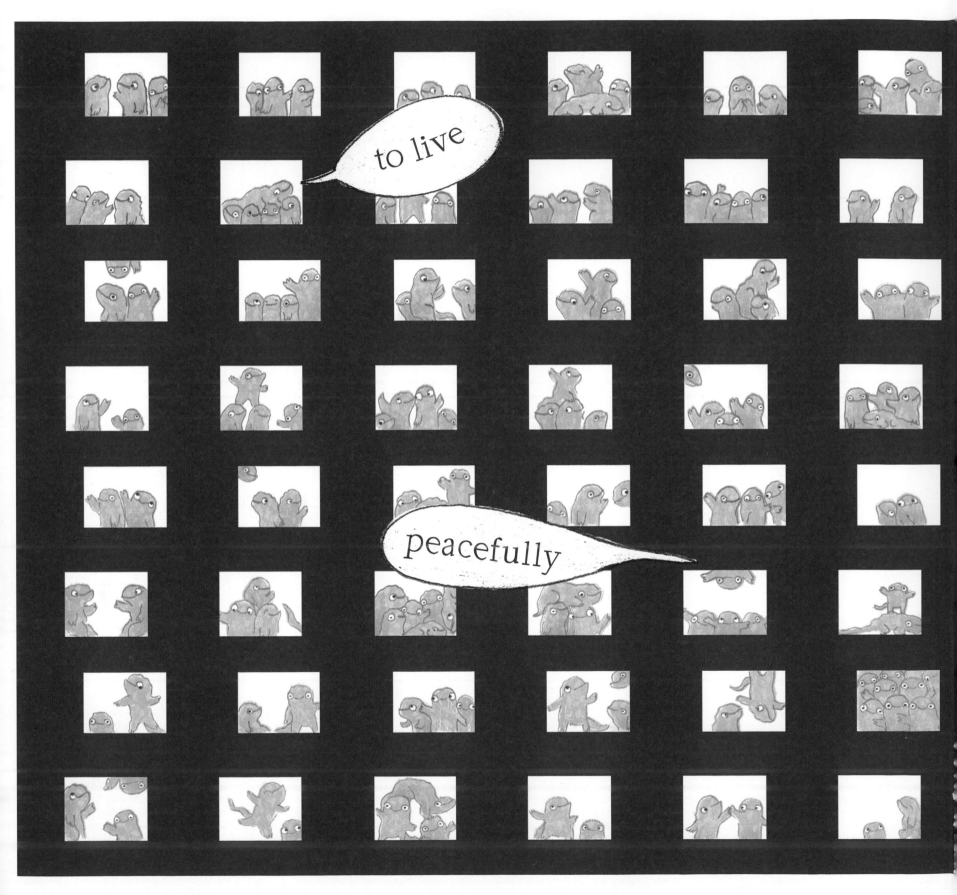

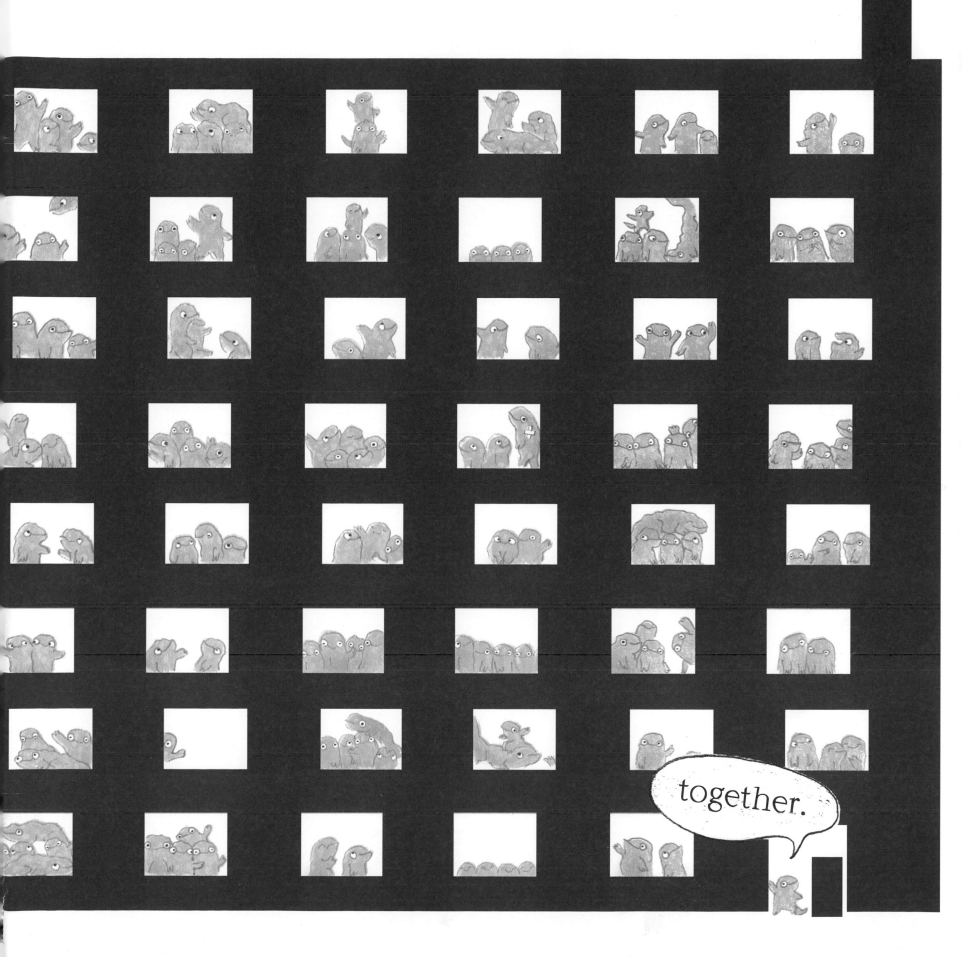

together.

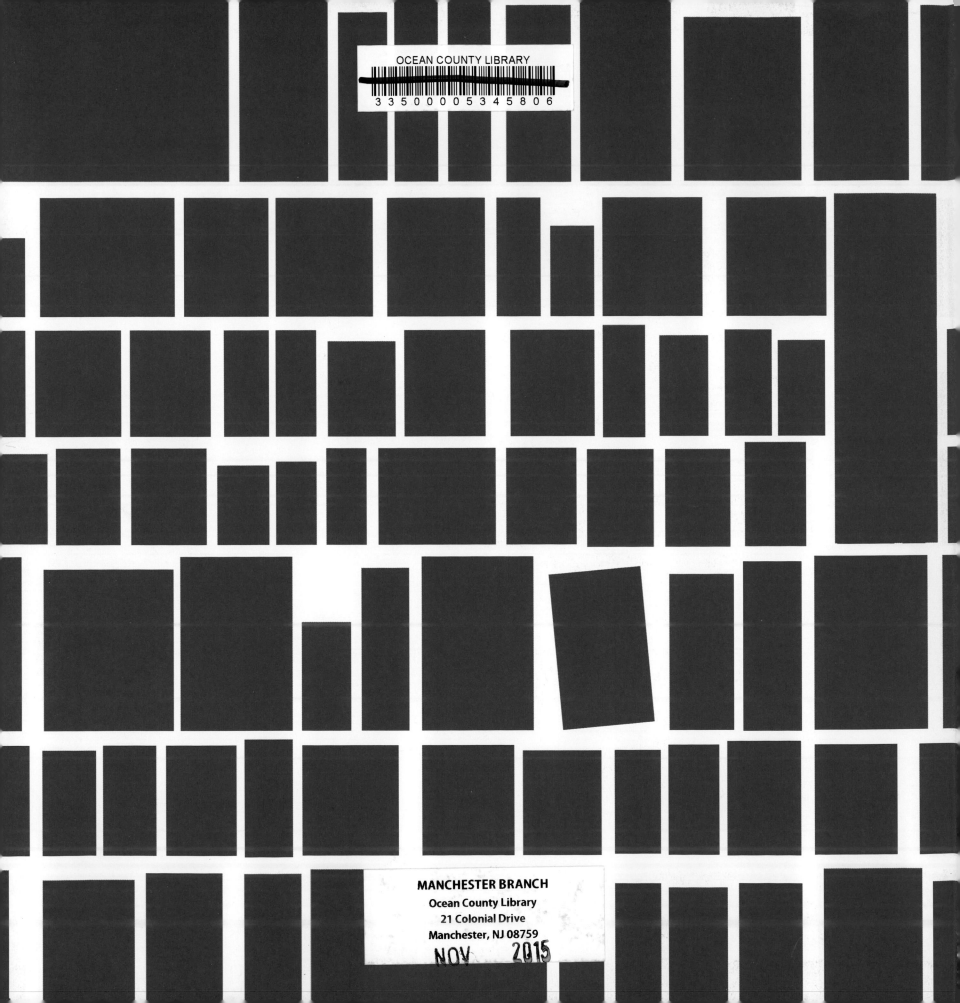